DOGS

By Jean Lewis
Illustrated by Turi MacCombie

Husky

GOLDEN PRESS • NEW YORK
Western Publishing Company, Inc., Racine, Wisconsin

For thousands and thousands of years people and dogs have been the best of friends.

In prehistoric times people shared their food and shelter with dogs. Dogs helped people hunt and guarded people's homes from wild beasts.

Today dogs are still our best animal friends.
Dogs work for us...

Border Collie

and protect us.

Mastiff

Dogs entertain us...

Poodle

Springer Spaniel

and love us.

Just as people are not all alike, dogs are not all alike, either. Some have long hair...

Afghan Hound

and some have short hair.

Boxer

Bedlington Terrier

Some dogs have curly hair.

There are even dogs
with no hair!

Mexican Hairless

Irish Setter

Collie

Basset
Hound

Springer Spaniel

Wheaten Terrier

Pomeranian

Japanese Spaniel

The different kinds of dogs are called breeds.
There are more than one hundred breeds of dogs
from all over the world.

The Samoyed comes from snowy Siberia, where it helps look after reindeer herds. Its coat is extra thick to keep out the cold.

The Lhasa Apso comes from Tibet. Though it is small, the Lhasa Apso is a good watchdog because of its keen hearing and shrill bark.

The St. Bernard is from Switzerland. For hundreds
of years St. Bernards rescued people caught in
mountain storms or buried by avalanches in the
snow-covered Alps.

The Irish Wolfhound, from Ireland, is the biggest dog in the world. It can grow to three feet tall and weigh more than 120 pounds.

The smallest dog in the world, the Chihuahua, comes from Mexico. A full-grown Chihuahua weighs only six pounds and can sit in a person's hand.

All dogs give us love and companionship. But some
do special jobs for people.

Seeing Eye dogs are trained to guide blind people
safely through city streets.

The Golden Retriever makes a fine Seeing Eye dog.

Years ago the Dalmatian's job was to run ahead of horse-drawn fire trucks, barking to clear the streets of traffic.

Today Dalmatians still live in many firehouses. They are the fire fighters' favorite pets.

A dog can be your favorite pet, too, especially if you take the time to choose just the right dog for you.

Before you get a dog, decide which breed you'd like best. Then think about whether that dog would be happy in your home.

For instance, an Old English Sheepdog probably wouldn't like living in a small city apartment. Big dogs need lots of room to run.

With its thick, heavy coat, an Alaskan Malamute might not be comfortable living in a very warm climate.

A dog show is a good place to see
many breeds of full-grown dogs.

The public library has books that show many different breeds of puppies.

The library also has books that tell you how to take good care of your dog.

One of the best places to find a dog is at an animal shelter.

Shelters have purebred dogs and mixed breeds, puppies and full-grown dogs. Each one of them needs a home just as much as you need a dog.

Mixed
Breed

Doberman
Pinscher

Mixed Breeds

Beagle

Mixed
Breeds

Malamute

Mixed Breed

No matter what kind of dog you choose, remember always to love it, care for it, and treat it like the best friend it is!